AF407442

A DAY TO REMEMBER

CHAPTER ONE

"When I grow up I will make sure this village suffers for treating us as if we are dogs and I will make sure I repay you handsomely for going through pains because of me." I bravely said while directing a gaze at my helpless mother.

"You will do no such thing my son. "My mother politely replied. She was sitting opposite to me as she held my right hand with her two hands. "When you grow up you will not help to destroy your village rather you will help to build your village. Is that right I nodded twice without a word.

She continued, "When you pray to maltreat people when you grow up, God will not answer your prayers let alone giving you money to carry out such evil intentions. But when you pray to help the needy ones should you be rich, God will make sure you become rich because He knows your intentions are pure and humanly. Also learn how to pay evil for good. Please take note of this my son; anyone who wishes to be useful to his country does not pay evil for evil. Did you hear me?" "Yes mama" I replied. " Now go and dress up let's leave for the farm" "Ok mama" I stood immediately and changed into my farming clothes.

My mother and I seemed to be the poorest family in Iheeme village. We were treated as a rags and commoners in the village. My name is Emeka. I am Ten years old. I was single handedly trained by my mother since I was told my father died when my mother was five months pregnant. We lived inside an old hut that seemed ready to fall either today or tomorrow. It was too difficult for my mother to raise me since my father had left her with nothing, not even a farmland.

I was very humble and energetic boy who could never let my mother suffer alone. My mother purchased a farmland on a yearly basis from Adaku who had many farmlands. My mother had been working so hard to make sure she meets up with the price demand from Adaku. If she fails to meet up; the farmland would immediately be taken away from her. One thing my mother had never thought of doing was to allow me hawk despite our awful situation. I had been very helpful to her. I almost followed her to everywhere she goes. I was very close to her as a new born baby is to her mother.

It was a huge fun farming alongside my mother. We were very busy getting rid of weeds around crops. We worked, rested and when it was around 5pm we returned back home. The next morning, as early as 7:15am my mother had already awoken to prepare breakfast. She had already made fire with a pot of yam boiling on top. She wasn't expecting me to wake up yet because I slept late last night. The weather was very cold which made me wear long sleeve. I dizzily made to the back yard and found her cooking.

"Good morning mama". "I greeted and yawned.

"Good morning my son." She politely replied. "I wasn't expecting you to wake up by this time. Did you sleep well?" "Yes i did mama". I replied. " Why did you have to wake up this early to cook mama ?" "What are you cooking?" "Porridge yam. Do you like it?" "Of course you know it's one of my favourite foods" She was sitting close to the pot of yam boiling on top of fire, she adjusted some fire woods and turned back to me; "my son please do not be offended I am sending you out this early morning; would you go inside and collect ten naira from my purse so you can rush down to mama Mbakwe's shop and buy me pepper. I forget there is no more pepper in the house." " Ok mama ." I quickly went inside, collected the money and made for mama Mbakwe's shop to get the pepper. While on the way, I met an elder who just passed me from behind, I greeted him but he focused his gaze towards his direction and didn't look back to know who greeted him let alone responding to my greeting. Maybe I was not audible enough so he could hear hear me or maybe his whole attention was focussed on where he was going. I concluded.

It startled me the way another elder who was coming in front of me scolded me within that range of time I greeted him. He warned me seriously not to greet him again so I don't afflict him with my evil existence. As if that was not enough, I met two children I considered my age mates, they began to stone me and called me all sorts of names. I became maladjusted when I got to mama Mbakwe's shop and she chased me away like a mad person. I shed tears and ent back home with frustration. I never wanted my mother to notice I was crying, therefore I dried away my tears. Despite my effort to stop crying, yet tears kept gushing out from my eyes. My mother scurried to me when she saw me coming; she comforted me, dried away my tears and took me inside.

CHAPTER TWO

It was 2: 45pm the following afternoon. The sun had positioned itself well on the sky and very harsh on people. I was hurrying to the house as regards to a cutlass we forgot at home when we got to the farm. On my way I met the same two boys who bullied me yesterday as they came towards me. They had started picking up stones from the ground and preparing for the same similar action they exhibited yesterday. We were still separated by distance. I was preparing for my own unique action as I bravely march forward towards them to reduce the distance. I dodged about three or four stones they threw on me but only few were able to land on my head until I faced off with them. I first give the first boy a very deserving blow on the nose and so was the second boy. I jammed their heads together and push them inside a nearby bush. I took a handful of sand from the ground and fed them with it one after another. When they staggered up, I posed properly for a fight as I waited patiently for their own retaliation. It surprised me the way they took to their heels without looking back. I dusted myself and continued my journey to the house.

At about 5pm same day, it has never been long we came back from the farm trying to shower, eat and rest for tomorrow's market. We quaked as a particular voice from outside continued in a grumpy manner. We emerged outside to see who the person was, behold it was Mazi Ndu and his son; father to one of the boys I beat up this afternoon. Look at what your child has done to my son. "Mazi Ndu grumpily said as he exposed his son's body to my mother on the areas he sustained bruises including his nose. Oh my God !" My mother shouted in deprecation. "Emeka did you do something like this?" She tried to touch the boy to

show some concern but Mazi Ndu shouted at her immediately.
"Taah....!" He quickly drew his son back. "Don't touch my son. Like mother like son! Evil woman! You are asking this taboo son of yours if he did beat up my son. I am now a liar. A complete titled man of Iheeme land . Igwe must hear this!
"Mazi Ndu please calm down it hasn't gotten... " My mother's polite speech was interrupted by the gruffness of Mazi Eke from a very close distance.
Where are that evil woman and her evil son Emeka? Mazi Eke grumpily said as he approached with his own son. "Ok you"re already outside.

Look at what your evil son did to my humble son." Showing the area his own son sustained bruises to my mother. I was standing while gazing at them like moron. I wasn't even showing concern to their complaints. I was only touched when I noticed my mother had started shedding tears. "Why did you have to beat them up Emeka; what happened? My mother asked with tears on her cheeks. "I am sorry mama but they keep looking for my trouble." Tears slowly roll down my cheeks. " I met these boys on my way going to buy pepper you sent me the other day; they bullied me and as if that was not enough they stoned me. I didn't retaliate because I wasn't in a good mood. Today as I was going home as regards to the cutlass we forgot at home, I met them on my way again; they stoned me and started calling me an evil child."   "Are you not an evil child?" The rhetorical question came from Mazi Ndu. " May be he's never been told that his existence is an abomination to this land. Mazi Eke added."But excuse me o..., Mazi Ndu I wonder if you're having the same thought as me. How can a little boy of Emeka beat up two boys who are a year older than him and keep them in this kind of condition? I disagree. It takes someone to be a witch or a wizard to do that."

"Concur!" Supported by Mazi Ndu.
"And we have to act fast before this boy kills every child in Iheeme Land." He pointed directly at me and focused his gaze toward me. "I'll personally make sure your life is cut short! It's a promise. " He threatened me and they all left through the same direction. My mother drew me closer to her bosom, comforted me and took me inside as we continued crying.

What happened today will forever remain in my heart. I pray I have the heart to forgive because the heart has been severely broken by my own people. Cogitation of my existence took away my sleep this night. I've been cogitating on what Mazi Ndu and Mazi Eke said about me. Could I be evil? Am I truly an evil child? But I've neither noticed any diabolical power in me nor exhibited any abnormal character. But why do my people keep calling me an evil child? Why did Mazi Ndu threaten to cut my life short? What could that possibly mean? These questions are beyond my experience and too difficult for me to answer. Therefore I reserved them for my mother to answer when she wakes up because she seemed to have finally forgotten what happened.

The time was 1:51am early morning, yet I couldn't sleep. I was sitting on a mat busy gazing at my mother who was lying on the same mat with me catching a good sleep.Little did I know she was having the same cogitation as me until she turned to me with a hiss of depression coupled with a question, "Why are you not sleeping Emeka? Does it have to do with what happened yesterday?"
"Yes mama, Is there anything I need to know about myself you're not telling me? Why is everybody calling me an evil child including my fellow children? Am I really evil mama?" I inquisitively asked.
"Sssh...," she closed my mouth with

her one finger. " Don't ever say something like that again my son. God forbid should you be evil! You are not evil my son and can never be evil." "Then why is everybody calling me an evil child?" " In no distant time you'll be fed in full details what happened. But now isn't a good time to talk about this. Thank God you have a brave heart as your father. You have to sleep my son. "She convinced me to sleep but it took me a very long time before I could do that.

CHAPTER THREE

Darkness had finally paved way for daylight with a little thunderstorm on the sky. There was no sign of early morning sun which meant that the weather was so misty. Elders in council were already seated in Igwe's palace deliberating on issue that has to do with the development of the village. Countless number of times they had written to the local government telling them to come and construct our roads and perhaps invite foreign or local investors in our village. Since the Local government could not attain to their needs they went ahead to write directly to the state government as they were referred to their local government council.

They added that if only they had any prominent speaker or representative in the government or better still their own local government all these breach of protocols wouldn't have existed. After few hours of deliberation, my matter was presented by Mazi Ndu and each of the elders articulated contemptuously about it. They all knew the evil that surrounded my birth. Even my fellow children seemed to know about it. I had never been told anything by anybody not even my mother; therefore I counted myself innocent of whatever evil they may hold against me.

It is a surprise that the fowl should hold a grudge against the pot instead of the knife that killed it. Even if there was any evil surrounding my birth was I the cause? Did I create myself? Why would they treat my mother and I like animals? They believed my existence is a calamity in the land of Iheeme.

"Magi! Magi!! Magi!!! Two hefty men on their security outfit showed a total disregard the way they shouted my mother's name as they approach our compound. When my mother came out from inside the hut to see who the callers were, behold they were Igwe's security men. Her whole body began to shiver. "Igwe summons you to his palace right away." The first security man disclosed.

My mother who tied wrapper around her waist demanded to go in and change into something better but her request was disrespectfully discarded by the second security man. "You worth nothing before the villagers; even if you are naked, you are going with us this minute." He dragged her out as the first security man prodded her with his right hand into movement. My mother was silently shading tears as she was being poked and prodded to Igwe's palace by the two security men. I woozily came out from inside the hut with tears flowing down my cheeks and watched them poked my mother until they were out of my sight. I wish I had an evil power to destroy these men. I pitied my mother for going through these pains and suffering because of my existence.   I shouldn't have existed! Our troubles never come single; it never rains but it pours. I had severally had the thought of committing suicide but I was advised by mother to be brave even when facing the highest difficulties. My mother was given the last prod into Igwe's palace. She stood fretfully and shamefully as regards to the wrapper she tied around her chest. She avoided a gaze at already seated Igwe and the Chief Priest. "Igweee......!" She humbly greeted. "I smell evil!" Chief Priest began with a wry visage. "Evil.....! I smell evil in the land of Iheeme! Unrelenting calamity is about to befall this land Igwe!!". "Magi." Igwe called out. He was being fanned from the two sides by his bodyguards. "Yes Igwe" My mother humbly replied. "I hope you still remember our agreement with the gods?" "I still remember Igwe." "I'm sorry to tell you that the gods have changed their mind. They are impatient to wait till the time they requested for the child. They have demanded for the sacrifice in the next four Nkwo market days. As you have heard from the Chief Priest that great calamity is about to befall our land if we fail to offer the sacrifice. You may leave now. "Igwe concluded.

My mother cried like a baby. She left without uttering a word. She knew the decision was from the gods. The clock struck 1:15pm same day. My mother came back beyond the pale. I was already seated at the backyard cogitating. I stood up immediately with palpitations and fixed my gaze at her but couldn't go to embrace her. She was really in a dazed state. She embraced me while sitting and made me sit on one of her laps. "Why did Igwe summon you to his palace mama?" I questioned. To my surprise I saw tears flowing down her cheeks. I became very sorry and pitiful because I thought I've aggravated her mood with my question. "It's nothing my son." She dried her tears. "He only warned me about thee incident that happened between you and those boys." "I'm sorry Mama," I began with words of apology. I'm sorry you have to go through this embarrassment because of me. I'll never fight again. I promise." "It's alright my son. But I still want you to be brave as your father no matter what happens." "I will mama." "Good boy. Now go and get me a bucket of water to take my bath. Have you taken yours?" "No Mama."I replied. "And I'm sure you've not eaten anything as well. Am i right?" I was already on my way to get her bucket of water to take her bath when she threw that question and I answered from a distance;"yes mama."

"Oh my God! Do you want to starve yourself?" That was a rhetorical question that required no answer. She stood up and made inside after me. Many thoughts occupied my mother's mind but she didn't know how to let it out. That brings me to a quote by Ugo-Bright Victor which says, "Be careful not to swallow your thoughts, your life might be inside." Of course my mother had swallowed her thoughts a lot and I pray her life doesn't follow. It's always unfair to swallow your thoughts and die silently when you've got someone confidential and reliable to discuss your problem with. For sure my mother can rely on me. She was my best friend but the reasons that made her keep so many things from me were best known to her. She always come with an excuse that I was still a little boy. She had promised to tell me when the time is right but I could see her being uncomfortable every minute of the day.

CHAPTER FOUR

It was 8:07am the following morning. The weather was very bright and the sun had already appeared but not too harsh on people. Leaves and tiny branches of trees were being blown around by wind. Goats bleated,birds chirped to its different tones, cock crowed and noisy hens with their chicks moved from side to side in search of food. My mother and I had already prepared to leave for the market. On my head was a basket of vegetable leaves and my mother was carrying a big plastic bowl containing tubers of yam. "My son,' we stopped for a while as she talked to me."I've been waiting for you to come of age so I can tell you what I've been keeping behind you for years. But since things have turned out to be this way I think it's time I unveil to you the mystique surrounding your birth and how your father died. But that should be reserved till we come back ok?"

"Ok Mama." I nodded in agreement. The thought of the mystique surrounding my birth and how my father died gave me palpitations. I became completely agitated. The hunger of going to market left me immediately. My legs became weak on the ground. My level of fear continually increased every second. What am I afraid of by the way? I could never answer that question. I pretended so my mother would not notice my state of discomfort.

Just about to exit our compound, Mazi Ndu who was carrying his dead son led a group of youths and also with them were minority of teenagers and children of my age. Some were holding leaves by different inscriptions on it- *THE EVIL CHILD MUST DIE ! EMEKA MUST DIE ! KILL NO MORE THE EVIL CHILD!* And many other unmasked inscriptions. They sang enigmatically as a sign of protest and shorten the distance between them and us. My mother and I became practically maladjusted. Our gaze at each other clustered. They finally came closer, Mazi Ndu dropped his dead son on the floor and laid inanimately. As Mazi Ndu was about to talk, the youth leader gestured the group to quietness. "This is your fellow child whom you kill with your evil power. " He started with a misty-eyed. "I've brought him for you to feast on his dead body since you're a vulture. Since ever you beat him up he has been struggling with his life until his

death. Maybe you were asked to bring him to your kingdom, why not take two of us with you now?'
My mother and I became helpless. We cried like babies. Death should come now because I've given up on this life ! I don't want to live anymore ! I wish I was the boy who laid inanimately on the floor. Isn't it better to die than to live this way? This life doesn't worth living. I wish I hadn't existed in this world ! I know my mother must be thinking the same thing too.

The youth leader faced the group and began with words of desolation. "We all know that this woman and her son are evil and do not deserve to live in this land. Or should we let them live and continue to kill us ?" The group shouted simultaneously. "Noooo!". Youth leader continued." When a witch woman wakes up very early in the middle of the night and begins to search for her wrestling belt under the bed, you ought not to be told that she is looking for her pot of charm to go and negotiate with surugede the spirit wrestler. And if surugede requests for a wrestling competition and she fortunately wins, that means, she is going to be sent to an exile with terrible and mysterious boils and skin pores. But if unfortunately she lose out the completion, that means she's going straight to hell to confront devil himself for more wrestling."

The youth leader proceeded to pushing down the goods on our heads respectively. My mother was forced to back the dead body as she was being poked and prodded. I was beaten and prodded by everybody to Igwe's palace. Mazi Eke was revealed with his son in the shrine appealing with Chief Priest to fortify his son against death. He told the Chief Priest that the first target is dead and he wouldn't want his son to die as a second target. The Chief Priest after saying some enchantments gave him a charm his son will always have in his pocket anywhere he goes.

We finally arrived in Igwe's palace. We were forced to sit on the bare floor after releasing the dead body from my mother's back. We had sustained bruises and injuries that made us uncomfortable sitting on the floor. Igwe on hearing the protest song was all about. He saw us sitting on the floor in despair as if we're going to die in the next three minutes. He apologized to the group to ease their grief. He also made them understand that we are food for gods in the next three weeks and we don't deserve to be treated the way we did because the gods might get angry. He finally pleaded with them to dismiss to their various homes and also assured them that the matter will be meticulously handled.

Youth leader emerged before the group. "The Igwe has spoken and he has spoken well. We shall all return to our various homes but if in the next three weeks this evil child is not destroyed we shall all return herein Igwe's palace with more serious protest. And he must die by our unanimous hands! Youth.....!" "No Nonsense!" The group of youths echoed. They began with their protest song and left in group. Igwe shook his head and made inside the palace with Mazi Ndu. Four guardsmen came out in no distant time and took us away.

CHAPTER FIVE

Already seated in Igwe's palace were elders in council. They gathered to deliberate on issue concerning me and my mother. Already standing with words on his lips was Mazi Ndu. " My son died because he was beaten by that evil child who calls himself Emeka. This nonsense has already gotten to our nerves and we must act fast to put an end to it before it becomes too late. I am very much convinced that this boy is not ready to stop until his mission is completed. Take it or leave it, he's not going to stop until we're all dead. His mission is to destroy this land." He got seated.

Mazi Eke stood. "Mazi Ndu has spoken wisely like the gods. Even my own son has been battling with his life since after he was beaten by that evil child. I've taken him to Dibiammuo the great one yet the sickness continues. Shall we continue to fold our arms and watch our children die one after the other?" "Aru....! Tufiakwa!" The council of elders responded with great disapproval and disgustedly snapped their fingers.

"I've heard you all. " Igwe started" But the question is, what do we do since the boy is still going to be served as meal to the gods in the next three Nkwo market days?" Mazi Ibe cleared his throat and stood up. " The truth is that the gods are always hungry. Even if the boy is sacrificed to them right now I don't think there would be any complain from them. "He got seated. Mazi Eme stood. "Mazi Ibe has spoken excellently well. Even the gods appreciated what is good. Let's destroy this boy now before he destroys our land." He got seated. Mazi Okon stood. "You all have spoken well like elders you are. But I also deem it necessary we employ the opinion of Chief Priest before we come to a conclusion." He took a gaze at everybody as they all nodded in agreement. They were all distracted and fixed their gaze at the only entrance door of the palace while the chief priest entered with his staff being struck on the floor each time he made a step.

"The gods shall never be forced to eat when they are not hungry. " The chief priest said as he drew closer to the elders in council."It is equivalent to a mother trying to force food into her baby's mouth when she knows very well that her baby is not hungry. The baby cries but the mother doesn't know the outcome of the cry. It invites pain and sorrow into the home. It'll cause more harm and sorrow to the land of Iheeme if the gods are forced to eat. The boy and his mother should be enclosed in a cage and must be served food only but once daily until next three Nkwo market days when the gods shall desire to feast on the evil child. The gods have spoken! He continued with his enchantment and exited the palace. Minus the brain and count the head useless. To say my mother and I are half dead is an understatement because we're already in the land of the dead. We had been humiliated, disgraced and dishonoured by our own people. "The gods shall never be forced to eat when they are not hungry."The chief priest said as he drew closer to the elders in council. "It is equivalent to a mother trying to force food into her baby's mouth when she knows very well that her baby is not hungry. The baby cries but the mother doesn't know the outcome of the cry. It invites pain and sorrow into the home. It'll cause more harm and sorrow to the land of Iheeme if the gods are forced to eat. The boy and his mother should be enclosed in a cage and must be served food only but once daily until next three Nkwo market days when the gods shall desire to feast on the evil child. The gods have spoken! He continued with his enchantment and exited the palace.

Minus the brain and count the head useless. To say my mother and I are half dead is an understatement because we're already in the land of the dead. We had been humiliated, disgraced and dishonoured by our own people.

We were enclosed in a cage for the

past one week and we seemed to have been brainstormed because we can't even think of anything else than crying. Even dogs received better treatment than we do. Sometimes we were being served food remained by dogs. I had on several occasions thought of committing suicide but my mother kept telling me,"be strong, be strong, be strong!" I am tired of being strong, I really want to end it now because I know my mother is suffering because of me. An innocent woman!

Life is worthless without joy! There was never a day I experienced joy in my life. My life is worthless. I don't deserve to live! It is two days and we have never been served any food. I became very hungry that I thought I was going to die. Even my heart was so strong and open to receive death but the question remains; "Where's the death?" It has refused to come and take me. I never believed my mother could be this strong. She's the reason I'm still living. Another one week had gone and itt was just four days remaining for the gods to feast on my body. I was so strong knowing that all of us will eventually die someday. What happens to my mother after my death remains my daily question. She would definitely not survive it. I pitied her always. I wish I could know the mystique surrounding my birth before I die but how do I ask my mother knowing her state of agony was beyond description. I never knew she was thinking the same thing as well. She had always wanted to tell me but she was afraid if I was really in the mood for that. She finally voiced it out after gathering the courage.

"Emeka I know now isn't the right time to start saying this" My mother finally said. "My conscience wouldn't let me keep this secret to myself even when I know you will die soon. 'She cried deeply and wiped her tears away. "However, I deem it necessary and important you know the mystique surrounding your birth. For I know with this confession your soul will feel free and joy after your death." We both shed tears like babies. She continued. "It was never your fault my son. But please have it in mind that you will never take vengeance to the spirit world or anywhere you might be going."

She was distracted by the protest song heard inside Igwe's compound by the youths of the village. Just the fear of the protest song gave us palpitations. What could have happened again? Everybody really wished me dead, even my fellow children. In no distant time two guardsmen came to take me away, I was crying and calling my mother to save me. My mother bitterly cried and pleaded on my behalf but she couldn't save me. They brought me before the presence of the youths of the village. I was brutally beaten and mercilessly stoned by the youths till I almost died. "Oh God" I have suffered, please let me die!" I cried out. Even if I was an evil child, do I have to suffer this way? What was my offence this time around? Nduka, the son of Mazi Eke is dead! I beard the consequence of any death that occurred in the land of Iheeme even the death of a chicken. I suddenly became death that killed people. At night, I was carried back into the cage. My breath was gradually seizing and my eyes were swollen that I couldn't see anything. I sustained bruises all over the body. My mother saw me and busted out a cry. She almost killed herself.

To her, this whole thing is getting out of hand and something must be done to end it all. The question remains, what can be done to end it all if not by killing ourselves. We never thought of escape since the security men never forget to lock the cage after dropping our food inside. The youth shad deplorably snatched from me the opportunity to know the mystique surrounding my birth before I die. My heart was full of sorrow and revenge. Could I ever forgive them? This is a question I would have to answer in the spirit world. If I should die now I'll make sure my spirit hunts every single thing in Iheeme land. Even an ant will suffer from my vengeance! This is what has occupied my memory since after I was brutally and mercilessly beaten by the youths.

The next morning, just three days before my death; villagers including Igwe and his council of elders were seated and every other person was standing in a circular form.We were positioned in the middle of the circle. After a brief murmuring and booing from the villagers, Igwe finally gestured them to a silent. He addressed them for a while before handling over to the Chief Priest to round off. In their speeches, they told the villagers to rejoice for peace is about to rein in the land of Iheeme as the gods are impatient to wait for the remaining three days before I could be sacrificed. Therefore they've demanded that the sacrificial be tomorrow. I shall die tomorrow! My mother almost cried her eyes out. My heart was full of agony. I could not cry because my eyes were still covered with bruises as regards to the deadly beatings by the youths. I prefer to die than to live a worthless life. A life full of sorrow, agony, hardship and most of all brutality! Tomorrow shall mark the end of my life! I grievously said inside of me.

CHAPTER SIX

It was a misty afternoon same day, 3:30pm. Leaves and some tiny branches of trees were dancing to the tone of the atmosphere. Already seated in the shrine was the Chief Priest. He was making some enchantments as a result of consulting the gods of the land. Mazi Eke entered in no distant time after removing his slippers. He remained standing and silent as nobody would interrupt the consultation of the gods. Chief Priest gestured him to sit after the consultation and requested to know what has brought him to the shrine. Mazi Eke, after praising the Chief Priest voiced out his reason of visiting the shrine. He cleared his throat and started off. "The dog that boasts of eating excreta must be sent to the toilet; *Kafa rijuo nsi afo! Eh.e,* is it not the same thing? They have boasted of being a witch and a wizard respectively. And they should be sent to the blood sucking world so they can fill their stomach with blood. *Kafa mijuo obara-afo*! What I mean is that, Magi should be sacrificed together with her son. If we kill a mother Lion that has been attacking the village and let specie live, that means we are still going to suffer by the hands of the specie when it matures. But if we totally eradicate the threat by killing the mother Lion and her specie that means we will go home and snore while sleeping."

"The gods are wiser than you are Mazi Eke" Chief Priest replied. "No one, I mean nobody, not even the greatest can change the decision of the gods. Go home Mazi Eke and burry that opinion of yours in the deepest of your mind. Otherwise the gods will hurt you don for calling them inferior." " But I never did call them inferior. I only...."Mazi Eke splutters out of fear.

"Gooo....!"Chief Priest gruffly butted in. Mazi Eke quickly and frightfully ran out of the shrine after gathering his slippers.

The time had gone from 3:30pm to 5:40pm. The sky was gradually turning dark.Though initially, the weather was not bright. Everybody was exceedingly excited knowing that their sorrows and the cause of their untimely death will soon be a thing of history by tomorrow morning. They were all getting prepare to witness the great event and of cause the evil child will soon depart from their society.

My awaiting death had become the talk of the town. I might give up the ghost before the sacrificial day being tomorrow the way I'm seeing myself because we had never been served food since three days now. They only managed to give us water which had become our only source of livelihood. However, the beatings from the youth were not helping my condition at all. The fear of what would happen to my mother after my death was the reason I am still living. Darkness had masterfully possessed the sky. The time was accurately 8:15pm. Everyone had seemingly gone far asleep except the guardsmen who were on duty of guarding us. Shortly and surprisingly to us, two plates of jollof rice without either meat or fish in it were brought before us by a guardsman. He unlocked the cage, kept the food before us, jammed the door, dropped a comment and then left. His comment was; "enjoy your last meal little wizard and prepare yourself tomorrow to meet the devil"! The comment got me into thinking whether the food was poisoned. "But I'm still going to die tomorrow after all" I said to myself. Without considering if the food was poisoned or not, I feasted on it because I was gradually giving up my breathe out of hunger. I was glad my mother also ate her food well. Of course she was as hungry as I was. The time became approximately 10:35pm. Nobody had come to check on us. Even the three guardsmen on duty were fast asleep. To our surprise, something that had never happened before occurred tonight. The cage was left unlocked by the guardsman who was here to drop food for us couple of hours ago. After several minutes of cogitation, we decided to escape since we know all the short-cuts in Iheeme land. Initially my mother suggested I escape alone but I insisted we must escape together. If fear existed, my mother and I didn't know. Even though there were strange sounds from different animals. We discreetly ran from bush to bush looking for the best route of escape. We avoided running through the major roads. We weren't actually running but it seemed like running to me because we were putting in our whole strength to be able to walk. My mother was holding my hand as we strenuously took a quick walk.

The time had gone from 10:35pm to 12:01am. There was no moonlight therefore we couldn't picture things clearly. I became weak and nearly gave up when my mother was bitten by snake. She sat on the bare ground swallowing her pain. She avoided shouting because she knew we might be implicated if she did. It must be painful. I noticed the pain on her face. I began to cry and so was she. She urged me to keep going but I disagreed and waited until the wound was dressed. She requested for a particular leaf, I got it for her; she applied it on the wound and tied it with a piece of cloth seen beside her. After some minutes of rest, we started our journey. The time was 2:00am. A hunter and possibly Mazi Eke spotted us from afar with his touch light and began to make a quick step towards us. My mother could neither run nor walk quickly. She suggested I run as quickly as my legs can carry me through the right direction so she can take the left direction in order to confuse Mazi Eke. Little did I know as a child that she had just confused me to escape alone. She knew if we took the same direction possibly we be captured by Mazi Eke. Therefore she decided to distract Mazi Eke with herself. The journey became more difficult for me walking alone in the bush. But do I have a choice? The answer is no! What would happen to my mother if captured by Mazi Eke was what occupied my memory. Even though I was a child but am still a man. I must not let emotions destroy my vision.

I became stronger after this thought and started my journey to nowhere. The time had gone from 2:00am to 5:05am. I seemed to have covered a far distance. I gave myself a little rest after discovering I was no longer in Iheeme village. I was now walking tiredly on a major road. Not longer had I walked, I heard a sound of a cup coming behind me. I turned back; it was a Toyota pick-up carrying some barrels of palm oil. I waved for the car to stop, luckily to me he stopped. Guess what happened? He gesture me to enter and we drove off.

CHAPTER SEVEN

7:00am same day. The weather was very bright and people had already resumed their daily routine. The morning sun was still struggling to appear. The Good Samaritan who picked me on the way finally stopped me on a very busy road/junction. He also gave me five thousand naira to add to his generosity. I came down looking ragged. I saw four buses loading passengers going to different cities. I clearly heard the loaders calling Enugu, Lagos, Abuja and Port-Harcourt respectively. After some minutes of cogitation on which bus to enter, I approached Abuja bus but unfortunately they mistook me as a little mad boy. I went to a bus going to Enugu and the same thing occurred. I finally landed myself inside Lagos bus after giving it a trial. We took off at about 8:01am after the bus was fully loaded with passengers.

While inside the bus, I had become tired of sitting and anticipating to seeing our bus land in Lagos. It was obvious that my bad odour was making everybody inside the bus uncomfortable but thank God they were all cooperative. I never knew from east to west was quite a far journey. I was very excited when I was told we've finally arrived Lagos. There was heavy traffic jam on the road so we got to the bus stop(Jibowu) at 7:45pm. I came down and carefully took a glance at different corners of the environment; it was totally strange to me. By the time of the night when everybody should be in their homes sleeping; everywhere was still very busy. If not as busy as the hell. Even though I've never been their but I've been told how busy fire in hell can burn.

I saw vehicles both big and small on a very long queue and each struggling to keep pace with vehicle in front to avoid being overtaken by a car from behind. I found I vary funny and was busy entertaining my eyes by watching the vehicles struggle with each other. I smile and almost got myself laughing for the first time since one year, when I saw a car hit by another car from behind. The owner of the crashed car violently dismounted from his car and made for the man who just crashed his car. The other man also came down, I was expecting the man who just crashed somebody's car to start with words of apology but the reverse was the case. He began to claim right as well, because of that, a heavy face-off arose between the two parties.

Just ten seconds of the face-off, they ere rounded by numerous numbers of people. I was surprised and began to ask myself where the people cam from. My excitement instantly turned to fear when I saw another scene being created by two rugged guys who started fighting themselves violently with broken bottles. I expected people to round them and quench the fight like they did to the other parties but nobody ever shoed up.   I became more frightened when I saw multitude of people seriously and cruelly running to my direction. Some had their bags thrown on the floor, some were running barefooted while some were even shouting and screaming as they ran. I quickly joined the race. Even the two fighters also joined the race.

Just a little while after the race had stopped. I took my time to dictate the cause of the running, believe me; nothing, not even an ant was chasing anybody. I became annoyed and blamed myself for coming to Lagos instead of Port-Harcourt.I never knew Lagos is as rascal as this. I became tired and started feeling pain again after the race. After an hour of searching for a place to sleep, I finally landed myself inside Young Shall Grow Park. I woke up as early as 6:00am the next morning. The first thing I did was o search my pocket to see if my two thousand one hundred naira(N2,100) was still there but believe me, I saw my money no more. I busted out a cry. How to eat this morning took possession of my thinking. The thought of where to get money to eat really made me thinking about my mother. Could she have been dead by now? Should I have escaped without her? Does this life really mean anything without my mother? Guilty conscience nearly dragged me to my early grave. Since weeping could not solve my problem, I stopped. However, I was becoming very hungry. The time had shifted to 7:58am. I just stopped crying but during my time of crying, I cried for almost an hour with deep voice. As a child nobody ever came to me to know why I was crying. I regretted this kind of city. I had gotten myself into. If I should cry for almost an hour and nobody care to know why I was crying as a child, I wonder who would care to give me money to eat in this rascal city.

I became jealous when I saw my fellow children backing their school bags going to their various schools. Some were carried by school buses from their various homes to school. I had a dream of going to school but was never privilege. I was busy moving from one person to another looking for money to eat this morning but unfortunately everybody mistook me as a little mad boy. If they continue to take me as a mad boy how would I succeed in this city? I tried in several ways to explain to them that I was never a mad boy but due to my bad odour and how tattered my clothes were; nobody ever believe me.   People almost got me frustrated but I didn't give up. I kept on using my last strength to beg for help. A very young guy of about twenty years finally helped me with one hundred naira(N100). I quickly rushed to fast food centre, ate fifty naira rice and saved the remaining fifty naira for next time. The money really gave me courage a lot. It showed me there are still people who are willing to help. I began to think big for myself. I must succeed in this city no matter how rugged it is.

I don't need to rely on people to eat. I'm too hard-working for that. Just two days of my stay in Lagos, I was popularly known as "the little mad boy". Even my fellow children called me the name. I was never angry with the name; rather it gave me more courage. I said to myself; one day everybody would know I'm not mad. It will soon become a history; this is what I believe.   I saw some people including children hawking sachet pure water, I bravely approached on of them, made inquiry where they normally buy it, I was directed and I took off immediately. Some minutes later, I got there and met people already buying. I went directly to the seller, made my request known to her but she furiously chased me out of her shop and because she thought I was a man boy. I went to the second shop and was chased away like a mad person. The third shop I entered also rejected me. I didn't give up. I went ahead to give the forth shop a trial but unfortunately the seller refused to sell for me install-mentally. I almost gave up. I exhaled in distress,made for a particular place and sat quietly to rest. This Lagos is nothing different from my village. It is dominated by wicked people. No one is willing to help. A city where there is a slim chances of survival for ordinary people. The rich get richer and the poor get poorer is generally Nigeria's code of conduct but mostly practiced in Lagos.

The thought of how to survive occupied my memory. Just about to leave after few minutes of resting; something said to me; "why not try somewhere else? You might be lucky." I decided to try again but not in that street again. No longer had I walked and sighted a young boy of about fifteen years old carrying a small bowl containing plastic and can soft drinks of different brands on the head. He told me everything I needed to know about the business including where they bought it after I have inquired from him. I headed to the place praying not to be turned down again, luckily for me the woman accepted to sell for me install-mentally after telling her my story, she asked me to repeat tomorrow because cold drinks had just finished. Not even my joyful mood can described how happy I was. Darkness gradually possessed the sky. Where to sleep became my problem since I was chased away from the Young Shall Grow Park. I finally found a place to sleep. Guess where? Ojuelegba under bridge.

CHAPTER EIGHT

I woke up around 6:15am the next morning. I bought five naira chewing stick in order to get my teeth brushed up. I had forty five naira left for me to spend. I was becoming hungry because I hadn't had meal since yesterday. I didn't want to spend the money unwisely therefore I waited for the time to come up so I can fill my stomach with biscuit. I hid the remaining chewing stick somewhere and started towards the shop. The place was a bit far but can be trekked. I trekked down to the place just to save cots. I got there around 7:30am. Normally you have to go there with your own bowl but I headed empty handed and fortunately for me the woman provided me with a bowl. Joy took over me and I left for hawking after loading the bowl with soft drinks of different brands. At the end of the day I came back without selling anything out of the fully loaded drinks. Nobody accepted to buy from me. Everybody mistook me as a mad boy. I was very hungry but I only had twenty naira left on me.How would I manage tomorrow if I should spend this money this night? I decided to sleep with an empty stomach and save the money for tomorrow.

I left for Iya Bola's shop the next morning at 7:00am. Thank God she didn't loose faith in me. She loaded another bowl of mineral water for me. I gladly left praying to sell at least some of it. But today became worst than I can imagined. Two naughty guys called *Alaye* collected Amstel malt each from my bowl while on my head. I became very excited because I thought they were going to pay me. It turned out something different when they asked me to leave without money. When I requested for money they gave me a sound slap on my check and tried to prove obstinate but I was given a better beating by them. All through my misunderstanding with them nobody ever came to know what the problem was.

I trembled on how cruel this Lagos is.It is really a collection of psychopathic patients. Darkness was gradually taking over the sky. I began to panic on what to tell Iya Bola. I finally gathered courage, made for the shop, disclosed what transpired between me and those Alaye boys. I expected she got mad at me but she only said a word to me "This is Lagos. Shine your eyes!" Does this kind of person really exist in this cruel city of Lagos? I was surprised. Hunger was already in me so I bought biscuit with my last twenty naira and filled my stomach with it. What tomorrow will bring is what I don't know but I pray it favours me. Just about to sleep, a young boy of nineteen years old, probably Agbero approached me,

"Hey wake up" The boy said and tapped me thrice on the leg. I quickly woke up in fear. For the past one week I've been seeing you occupying this duplex alone. Who did you pay your house rent to? Agent and agreement fees are paid directly to me but since you moved in I've not seen any money yet. Who did you pay to?" His voice was very coarse and harsh that I became confused. "I paid to.......... I paid to......." I stammered confusingly. "Paid to who? Speak fast let me go and collect my money from the person immediately before he spends the whole money." His voice was very harsh and loud. I bursted out cry."I paid to nobody" "Do you use to smoke weed?" He asked with his eyes widely open. "Yes sir but no sir. I didn't know you have to pay before you sleep under bridge" I confusingly replied in tears. "Ahh.....! He loudly shouted and began to quake vehemently. "You didn't know you have to pay before you occupy somebody's property? Is this a kind of joke or what? Or are you mad?" I quickly replied confusingly. "Yes I am mad but not too much sir. People call me little mad boy." "Shut up! I don't care if you are mad or not. At least you still speak with your senses. I am the caretaker of this duplex you are occupying and all house rent including agent and agreement fees are paid to me. The former occupant of this duplex was given quit notice because of his inability to meet up with his house rent. I will forgive you for not payin your house rent before packing in because you are a little boy. But do you have the money now?" "I have no money sir" "Look at this boy oo...! Do you think I am here to joke with you? I will treat your fuck up now if you don't comply." He ordered me to stand up, when I stood up, he searched me thoroughly and found no money.

"What is your name?" He asked

"Emeka." I replied

"How old are you?"

"Ten years old"
"I will let you live in this duplex alone on one condition." He ordered me to sit and he sat with me. "I will give you the opportunity to make big money by working with me. But my fear is that you are not a clever boy. Can you steal? He asked, focusing his gaze at my eyes.
"No sir. I have never stolen before" I bet you will become a professional thief"   "But I'm a new person in this Lagos sir."
"Try to be smart boy. You have nothing to worry about. Besides I've got your back. I run this city and make things happen in this city. I decide what happens in this Lagos o;

if you want to succeed you have to shine your yor eyes well o....! Just a day of business with me you will go home with the sum of ten thousand naira. Think of what ten thousand naira can do for you. You will probably change your clothes and most importantly feed well. Pick-pocket is not a crime in Lagos State. It happens to be one of the best and lucrative business in the city. Almost everybody does it. I will give you only but this night to think about it and we shall be living tomorrow morning for the park to commence work immediately. Shine your eyes!" He left.   Cogitation was the next thing I noticed in me. I was thinking what ten thousand naira could do for me. Perhaps God might want to use this offer to console me for all my misadventure. But stealing is never the way of God. What do I do since I have been unlucky since I was born? I was really confused. I finally made up my mind to follow him to wherever he may go tomorrow. Meanwhile he has threatened to stop me from sleeping under the bridge which he claim to be his property. I was never comfortable while sleeping. A particular quote by Ugo-Bright Victor kept repeating in my heart;"Learn to live life well otherwise life will learn leave you soon!" I always considered this quote each time evil thought came to exist in my heart. The quote has kept me going. I decided not to involve myself in such an evil act. I slept peacefully but mindfully because I would have to wake up very early in the morning.

I woke up around 5:46am, brushed up my teeth and thought it wise to leave the place before the boy comes. The road had already become busy as early as 5:46am. I wandered aimlessly from place to place waiting for time to come up so I can start going to Iya Bola's shop. I made for the shop finally around 6:58am. I waited for few minutes before Iya Bola came. She loaded the drinks for me as usual and left, I couldn't believe what today had brought. Not even a drink came back with me. I would have sold my container if it was placed on sale. I became glad because I made a little profit. Iya Bola was also very happy for my progress. I told her about the boy last night and she provided me with a place to sleep inside her shop. The time was 4:15pm; I wen to Tejuosho Market (Yaba) and bought myself a short and a T-shirt so people would stop calling me the little mad boy. Iya Bola was very excited to see me on a new dress. I left for hawking and also came back with good testimony. I sold everything.

CHAPTER NINE

My progress so far has boosted my effort. I became happy the way things were going. At about 8:05am I had already been on the road hustling. All this effort was for my mother. My plan was to bring her over to Lagos if at all she's still alive. I pray she remain alive. But my village people are very heartless. They might kill her in place of me. Let God judge them for their wickedness towards me and my mother. The time had clocked 1:47pm. I had only few drinks left to be sold. The sun was too harsh and I needed to rest. I began to trek to the back of a particular building. I had never been there since I started hawking. I've taken a long walk yet I've sported nobody. Not even a fellow hawkers who were desperate to enter any place provided they'll make sales. Besides, the environment was full of ventilations even though it was sticky. I never knew that nobody was allowed to enter there. I became afraid, anted to run back when I saw some group of hoodlums smoking weed, one of them spotted me and ordered me to come back shivering. "*Wetin give you moral to enta our cabal?* He questioned in Pidgin English.   I shivered." Nothing sir. I was looking for a place to rest."

"*If nobi say you be small boy, we for kill you hia.* The threatening came from another gangster ho was sitting and enjoying his smoke.

"I'll never come back here again sir, forgive me sir. "I apologized with misty-eyed coupled with great fear. "*Wetin you cari for head self?* "The question came from the first gangster who stopped me. He was also seated and smoking. " Mineral sir." I replied. "*De mineral no get name?*"   " I have only team, coca-cola, 7up, fanta, mirinda and mountain dew"

"*How many dey dia?*" "Seven sir. "I replied. *"Carry am come down"* He ordered. I quickly brought it down.

He asked few of his colleagues who were interested in the drink and ordered me to share it amongst them starting from him. He then asked me to sit down and have some rest. I sat down uncomfortably on a block seen by the side as I watch them smoke. Breeze was not helping my condition the way it was directing the smoke straight to my nostril. I didn't show any sign of discomfort so as to be recommended by them. I later got the recommendation from one of the gangsters who nicely remarked me as being a strong boy. I was busy thinking of my drinks and the money I had on me. They may refuse to pay me and might even rob me of the little money I had on me. Initially I took them as *Alaye boys*; but they turned out to be a group more dangerous than I thought. They were hire-killer! A group of gangsters who kill for money. Right before my presence they were plotting the elimination of the Surulere Local Government Chairman. I began to panic but I didn't let them notice my state of anxiety. I was surprised when I was asked how much my money was by the first gangster who stopped me. I disclosed the amount; he paid me and even asked me to keep the balance. I was dismissed and asked to come again next tomorrow. They seemed to have liked me. But it's dangerous associating with this kind of people. I thought.

I was full of thought as I headed to Iya Bola's shop. I was asked to come next tomorrow and not tomorrow because their operation would be carried out by 4:00pm tomorrow. I became confused on what to do. Should I tell somebody about this? "No" I disagreed after giving it a second thought. I might get myself implicated. I blamed myself for going there in the first place. Does God really want to use me to spare the life of this Surulere Local Government Chairman? But how do I do that? I was full of thought. I took the wrong direction on my way to Iya Bola' shop as a result of being in deep thought. I got to Iya Bola's shop, balanced my account and weakly made for a chair seen very close to the shop and sat down thoughtfully.

Darkness had successfully taken possession of the sky and I hadn't concluded on what to do tomorrow. I tried severally to force myself into sleep but couldn't. I was awake cogitating on the kind of action to take tomorrow. If I involve myself in this, I might get myself killed by those hire-killers. God..., I'm confused, what should I do? If I had known I wouldn't have gone there in the first place. Should I know about this and still allow the Surulere Local Government Chairman killed,I might die of guilty conscience. I didn't sleep all through the night. Around 5:30am, I brushed my teeth and took my shower. Darkness had giving way for light to take over the day. Iya Bola came and I was always the first to be served before others. I left for hawking. Around 2:00pm, I sold the last drink in my container. I now use a bigger container. I quickly started towards Iya Bola's shop still battling with my thought.

I bravely made up my mind on what to do. After making some inquires I started towards the Local

Government Building around 3:37pm. Due to traffic jam, I got there around 3:50pm I painted my face with a charcoal thus I wouldn't be recognized by anyone. On my head was a face cap I just bought to give my face a good cover. Chairman was informed about my visit after so many questions and delay from his security men. The time had shifted to 3:55pm. Because I insisted firmly on seeing the Chairman face to face, he permitted me into his office, I came with my face downward. "Yes little boy, so what do I...."Chairman was trying to question me and I butted in immediately. "Chairman you have only five minutes to escape from this building. Your life is involved!"I disclosed. He was still spluttering when I scurried outside immediately. When I discovered I had covered a little distance from the office but still inside the compound I took to my heels. Chairman glanced at his wrist watch; it was already 3:56pm. He scurried outside but couldn't see me again. He became more confused. On my way to Iya Bola's shop, I disposed the cap, washed away the charcoal on my face with water and later thought it wise to head straight to Tejuosho market to get myself a new dress instead of going to Iya Bola's shop first. Iya Bola was glad to see

me change into another dress when I came back around 5:30pm. It wasn't long I came back the radio annouced that Surulere Government building was attacked by fully armed robbers. Everybody around shouted and it became the talk of the moment. According to the announcement, only four people were killed.
I pray the Chairman doesn't follow among the four people killed so my effort wouldn't be waste. Radio came back again with the same news in thirty minutes time. It was announced that the target of the armed robbers was to eliminate the life of the Surulere Local Government Chairman but failed to succeed. It

was also said that the Chairman escaped before the armed robbers could get there. I chuckled from where I seated, my effort is not a waste after all. I became excited, now I can peacefully snore while sleeping this night.

CHAPTER TEN

Because of how misty today's morning is, it's undoubtedly clear there will be rain. The rain later came around 7:58am and didn't stop until 1:20pm. Neither I nor Iya Bola's other customers went for hawking today because of the rain. I wonder how the hire-killers would be feeling now. What if they found out I was the cause of their failure? Thy would probably skin me. I guessed.

I expected to hear from the newscaster on radio that a little boy masterminded the escape of the Surulere Local Government Chairman but such thing was never mentioned. Maybe the Chairman knew the dangers attached and decided to keep it secret. I was glad that such thing was never mentioned, otherwise the hire-killers will hunt me down. They were very kind to me that day but conscience couldn't let me watch them do what is inhuman. They asked me to come back but fear couldn't let me go. I wish I could go just in case they have another person in their agenda. Risky as it is, if you are afraid of taking chances, there is no way you can succeed: I bravely made up my mind to give them a visit tomorrow. I took off with a bowlful of mineral water the next morning. I thought today would be profitable like other days but it turned out to be something else. It had brought a very bad market to me. It was 12:00pm already, yet I was unable to sell up to seven drinks. I had become tired of walking around without seeing buyers. The bad market made me think of going to the hire-killers joint to see if they could buy from me. My feelings were more of agitation then that of guilt as I headed to the hire-killers joint. I finally got there. I was warmly welcomed by them. One of them asked me to share the remaining drinks amongst the interested persons. I did as they wanted it. I proceeded to sitting on a block seen beside me. I was cooling the pressure of the day with a fanta I received from them as a benefit of being in their gathering. They were discussing with their own personal terms to unable the second party understand their language clearly. I was wise enough to comprehend their discussion very slightly. You can't believe this. They were plotting the elimination of the state governor by 8:00pm today! I became shocked, they later paid and dismissed me. Should they succeed in killing the state governor, there'll be a great conflict and confusion in the state. It would definitely affect everybody in the state including myself. Fear gripped me even the more.

The time was already 6:00pm. I began to make some inquires on how to locate the governor's house. I knew it was very difficult to see the governor but I also know with determination and good effort you can achieve whatever you want. I started my journey to the governor's house around 6:45pm. I arrived at

7:15pm.

Commercial buses normally stop a bit far from the governor's house. Fear nearly discouraged me from continuing the journey but I gathered courage after some minutes and trekked down to the governor's house. On getting to the gate, a soldier with long gun halted me. He interrogated me and discovered I was eager and desperate to see the governor. The time had shifted to 7:40pm and there was no time left for me to spend. Other Soldiers, Policemen and Mopol rounded me and requested to know why I wanted to see the governor, but I insisted to see him in person.

After giving me a thorough searching, they tried to chase me away but I refused. The time had gone to 7:50pm. Only ten minutes left. I was telling them it's important I see the governor otherwise adversity will be the portion of this great city. They saw me as a little child; therefore none of them gave me a listening ear. After a convoluted disagreement amongst us, the governor who was on a convoy of about eight exotic jeeps accelerated slowly outside the compound saw what was going on and decided to hear from me. He was in the forth jeep.

"Good evening his majesty" I greeted

after approaching him.

"Good evening my boy, how are you?" He replied after he had wind down his door glass. "I am very well, thank you Sir." I replied."Ok. So what is it you want me to do for you?" He asked.

"I presume you are going for an executive meeting. "Yes I am. But how did you know that?" He surprisingly asked.

"You're not save Sir; you're about to be attacked by 8:00pm in johnson street. Some group of gangsters have plotted your death Sir, they are all armed beyond your imagination Sir. Your security men can never beat them. So I suggest you cancel the meeting Sir. But just in case you still want to test my trust worthiness you can quit going with them but let them go and see how they escape the attack. "But how did you know about this?" He confusingly asked. "Is not necessary Sir; I'm so happy to see you in person Sir. Good luck!" I ran out and stooped after remembering something else to tell him. I ran back. "Please Sir be careful with the people you dine with; especially Mr Kayode Kolawole. He is your worst enemy!" I ran speedily to the bus stop and entered a commercial bus.

The governor decided to test my trust worthiness; he dismounted

from his jeep and asked the rest to continue the journey on convoy. Not quite long they left; the news came to the governor. It happened as I said. No one on the convoy survived. I got to Iya Bola's shop at about 9:30pm; she had already locked the shop and gone. I slept outside.
One week later, I never knew I had been declared wanted by the governor. I was hawking as usual when a police pick-up (ford) stopped beside me and ordered me to stop. One of them quickly jumped down, carried my goods to the car and forced me to enter the car. They drove off with me. While inside the car, I carefully watched the

policemen and with them was one army man, possibly the first soldier who halted me when I wanted to find my way into the governor's house. I began to panic that finally I've gotten myself into trouble, I was ready to face whatever consequences because I knew I had done no wrong.

What I thought would happen was however entirely different from what happened. The governor was very happy to receive me into the governor's house. He appreciated my effort and told me after several investigations, the deputy governor being Mr. Kayode Kolawole was the one who plotted his death so he could become the governor of the state. He also disclosed that the deputy governor and the gangsters had been sentenced to life imprisonment. He put me through school, bought me an exotic jeep with numerous Soldiers, Mopol and Policemen accompanying me as an escort. As if that was not enough, he awarded me "The Most Popular Boy in The City!"   I became a hero who was published on many newspapers, showed on every TV station and my name broadcasted nationwide on all radio stations. 'The Little Mad Boy' now The Most Popular Boy In The City! I've achieved what many people who have lived in the city for years could not achieve.   I know it's not by my power but by the Grace of God. I vow never to live and see the needy ones suffer. I proceeded to find an organization called HOT'R' (Hunger On The Run!) Our mission is to eradicate poverty.

CHAPTER ELEVEN

One month later I headed to my village on convoy. Nobody recognized me again. I headed straight to Igwe's palace with my security men. Even the Igwe and the Council of elders could not recognize me. When I first came in with my security men, everybody bowed for me including the Igwe as a sign of respect. I now disclosed to them I was the evil child. They were all full of shame and guilt. I asked about my mother and I was told she was banished from the village since the gods rejected her as a sacrifice. I gave them an order to find my mother within twenty four hours otherwise I will declare state of emergency in the land of Iheeme. Three days later, I lodged in a hotel, a town that gave our village three hundred kilometers gap. It was 8:19am, I was inside my hotel room when my phone rang and I picked it up, it was the Igwe.

"Good morning Sir." Igwe's voice was

clearly heard.

"Yes good morning, who's this?" I asked.

"It's me Igwe Ochanga" He identified.

"Yes Igwe, have you found my mother? I inquired.

"Yes, We just found her. In fact she's with me now."

"Are you Serious? Wow.... I aborted the call immediately and happily jumped down from the bed. I sang and danced for while. I alerted my ascorts and we headed towards my village. Once in the village, I saw my mother and began to shed tears. Her look was just like a mad woman. She was full of surprises and began to shed tears too as we embraced ourselves. I quickly ordered the Igwe to permit her use his bathroom. After taking her shower, I ordered one of my security men to give her a good cloth to change into. She is the best mother in the wide world! She is my Idol! She is the reason I'm still living. There's something left for me to hear. I know you might be waiting to hear it too; the mystique surrounding my birth. Even though some would say it's no longer important or necessary since I've become successful already but to me it's something I've always wanted to hear.

I ordered Igwe to gather the Villagers

including the council of elders to the village square and he did as I ordered. Just as usually, they formed a circle. Igwe broke the law of silence as he open the speech"Good morning good people of Iheeme."

"Igweeee...." Villagers responded.

"We have a very important personality in our midst. He is the reason we have all gathered here in respect of his achievement nationwide. He is the founder of HOT'R'. I am also proud to announce that he is our son. It is a proud thing to say that such person hails from this village. His name is scattered all over the world; popularly known as the youngest minister or the most popular boy in the city. He is no other person than our son Emeka." The villagers became silent. They were all looking around to see the Emeka Igwe was referring to. Nobody expected my own Emeka but it turned out to be a great surprise to them when I came from nowhere with my mother to address them.

"Good people of Iheeme, I greet you all" I started with a greeting ."I know many of you cannot recognize me even while standing before you. In order to identify myself to your own best recognition I must use the name you all know me as,"an evil child!" Villagers screamed simultaneously. Shame was the next thing that appeared on their faces. I continued."The evil child everybody scorned and despised like a worm. The evil child that must die. The evil child that was tortured mercilessly by his own people. The evil child that was enclosed in a cage with his mother for whole three weeks. My mother was already in deep cry and so was I. Many who were affectionately hurt were also crying with us, even Igwe and the Council of elders were remorsefully shedding tears.

I continued."Does anyone know how it feels to be scorned, despised and rejected by your own people? People who are supposed to protect, you turned against you. Not only did everybody reject us but there was never a day you couldn't find one fault or the other in order to have us punished. Why? Oh we really suffered in the hand of the people who are supposed to be our people. You said I was behind the death of every single soul in this village. You accused me of killing them with my evil power. Come to think of it, I possessed such an evil power and refused to destroy this land for making us suffer the way we did. You made us suffer because of one useless tradition. This is absolutely insane! Now can anyone answer this question without sentiment; since

I've been away from this village hasn't anyone died?'   Nobody responded. I continued "I heard that Mazi Ndu is dead, why don't you accuse me of killing him too? I don't even know the reason I was called an evil child and I'm sure many standing here today don't know either. No one ever told me the mystique surrounding my birth yet I was being punished for that. I wanted my mother to tell me the story about the mystique surrounding my birth before everybody but the agony on her face showed she was never ready for that so I appointed Mazi Ibe to take up the job.
He remorsefully stood and began

with a faded voice."Your father was banished from Umunchi Village as a result of having his hands stained with blood. He ran to Iheeme for a refuge which is a great abomination according to our tradition. Several efforts made to eliminate his life proved abortive because of how brave, strong and powerful he was. He was so powerful that no warrior in Iheeme land was able to face him. Since ever he came to our land he became a noose on our necks. He started stealing our goats, fowls and other domestic animals. Strange things like premature death began to occur in our land. He killed without remorse anyone who question his unscrupulous attitude. We had five of our remarkable and reputed elders killed by him. One day we decided to employ the assistant of Umunchi warriors since they were more powerful than our warriors. But when they came, your father was nowhere to be found. Little did we know that your mother was the one who took him in. Before we knew he was harbored by your mother. Umunchi warriors had already gone back to their village and refused to come back again. We the council of elders though of what to do and later came up with a brilliant idea. We poisoned his food through your mother who claimed she was being used by your father. When we discovered your mother was pregnant by him some months later we decided to sacrifice her but the gods rejected her because of the pregnancy. We knew the child Magi was carrying would suffer because we regarded the descendant of your father an evil. We believed he would always give birth to a creature in his likeness. We agreed with the Gods to sacrifice the child when he is twelve years old."

"But you have all got it wrong, can't you see?" I began with misty- eyed.

"I was created to be opposite of my father. I was created to change the story of this village and not to

destroy it. Like my mum always told me., if you wish to harm others when you become rich, God will definitely make you nobody. But if you wish to help others when you become rich, God will definitely make you great. I share a different destiny with my father and that makes us different . You have judge me wrongly."
I was deeply shedding tears and so was my mother. Igwe apologetically knelt down, followed by the council of elders before the villagers. Should I forgive these people after all they have done to me and my mother? My mother also knelt down in apology asking me to forgive them. I couldn't just imagine my mother

kneeling down for me. She made me what I am tody. She is my Idol. I raised her up immediately and we affectionately embrace each other. Rapprochement reigned between me and the villagers. I made Iheeme Land the greatest of all neighbouring villages. I called the attention of government to our village, roads were constructed, companies, factories and industries built. pipe-bone-water almost in every compound, schools built in abundant, constant electricity and most importantly Local Government created. I rewarded Iya Bola by securing her a good office in the ministry of finance. I took my mother to Lagos and we lived happily together in the governor's house.

To you my readers, never you give up on yourself, that you are rejected by people or no one believes in you doesn't necessarily mean you are worthless or nobody. Keep working on what you believe in, when you fall,rise up and try again and again. God will definitely change your story someday. Always learn to live life well so life doesn't learn to leave you soon! Big-Solar has got a good quote here. "Be wise and live responsibly!"